A Snowman named just Bob

Written by
Mark Kimball Moulton

Illustrated by
Karen Hillard Crouch

ideals children's books™
Nashville, Tennessee

ISBN 0-8249-5860-8

First published in this format in 2003 by Ideals Children's Books
An imprint of Ideals Publications
A division of Guideposts
535 Metroplex Drive, Suite 250
Nashville, Tennessee 37211
www.idealsbooks.com

Previously published by Lang Books, Delafield, Wisconsin

Library of Congress CIP data on file

Printed and bound in Italy

10 9 8 7 6 5 4 3 2 1

For our treasured families and friends,
the moon, the stars, tiny little snowflakes,
carrots... each other...

...and all the innocent bystanders
who get caught up in the magic.

-Karen and Mark

Gladly presented to:

On this day:

from:

It was late
that one Thanksgiving
when Bob first
came to me . . .
a joyful day
of food and fun,
with friends
and family.

We'd feasted well, as I recall,
on Mother's fine-cooked fare,
then settled down to rest a while
and nap without a care. No one knew what was to be,
as daylight grew quite dim, that soon our lives
would change so much, simply because of him.

The weatherman reported that no snow was due that night,
but as we slept, the clouds rolled in, obscuring all the light.
And though that weatherman had tried, he never could have said,
just what was forming in the sky, directly overhead!

The Moon grew bright,
then disappeared,
then broke into a laugh.
The stars began to dance a jig,
the clouds just split in half.

In retrospect I do believe
that magic came that night—
no ordinary storm, you see,
could stir up such a sight.

The sky began to whip around,
then settled on its way.

The wind skipped lightly through the trees,
inviting me to play.

And late that eve,
there fell the first exquisite, tiny flake—

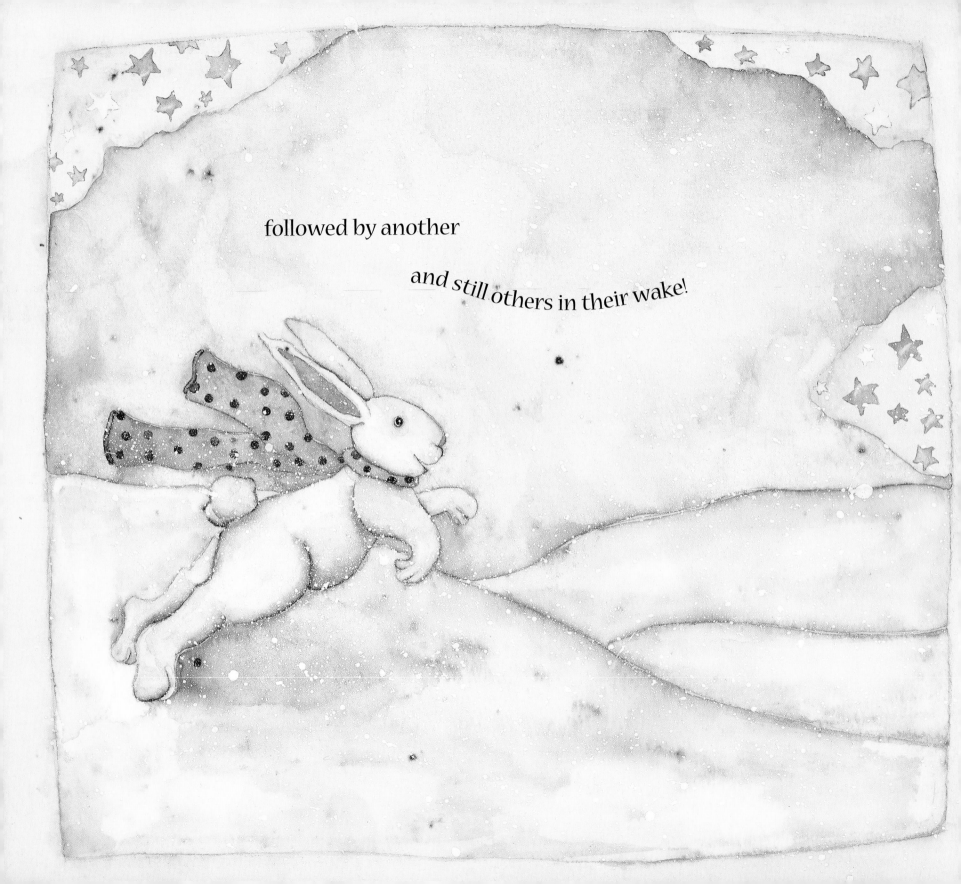

followed by another

and still others in their wake!

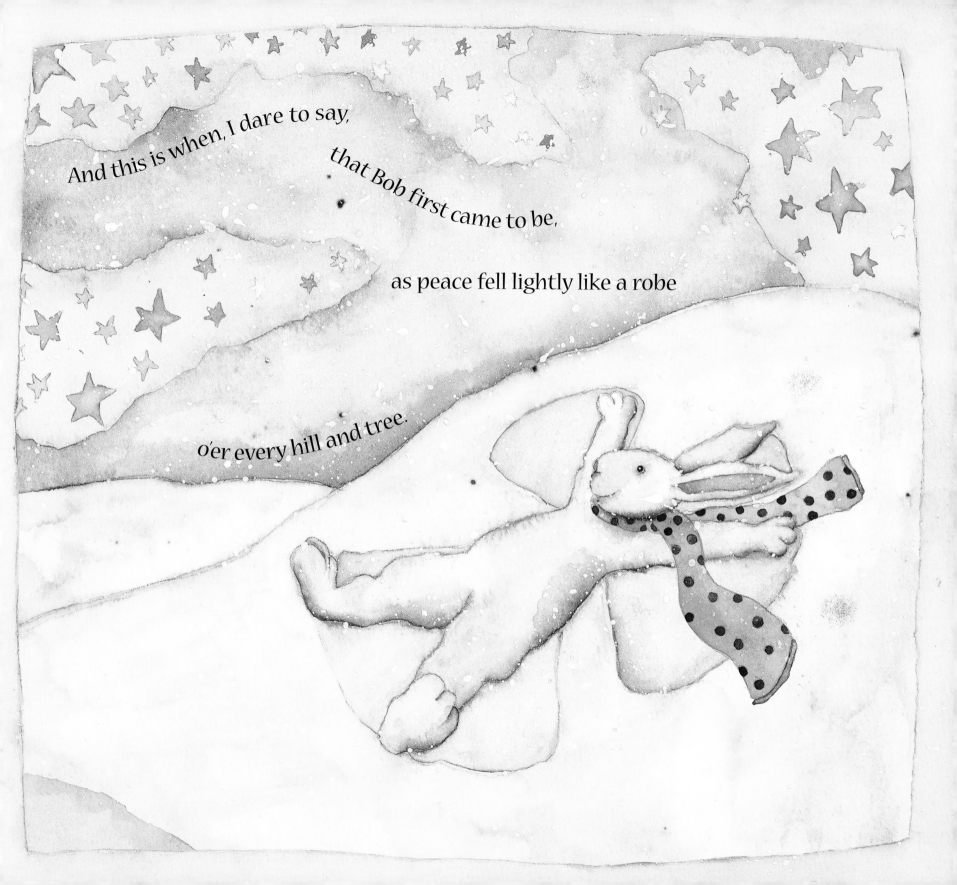

And this is when, I dare to say,

that Bob first came to be,

as peace fell lightly like a robe

o'er every hill and tree.

He fell upon my windowsill, he landed in my hair. He frosted all my neighbors' homes and blew throughout the air.

Just when it seemed the storm might pass, or at least be quite mild, the Moon came out and gave a wink and then stood back and smiled.

'Twas like he knew the answer to a real-life mystery— a delightful understanding that would soon be clear to me.

The snow took on an eerie cast—
first pink, then blue, then gold.
Then anxious little whirlwinds
leaped round my feet, so bold!

Suddenly, I heard Bob whisper—
his voice was soft and kind—
he asked me if I'd help him then,
if I was so inclined,

to gather up those many flakes
and roll them in a ball,
till he could be, and be with me,
in shape and form and all.

"But Bob," I cried, "I just don't know where you are in all of this!
'Cause all of you is everywhere throughout this snowy-ness!
You're scattered over everything! How do you recommend
that I gather all your goodness up and make a perfect friend?"

'Twas then Bob shared a secret,
and I knew just what to do,
for he whispered these few words to me
that I now share with you—

I ran into my mother's house
to wake those sleepy folk.
I bid them come and help me
to roll and pat and poke,
and build that grand ol' snowman
and do a right good job,
to bring to life
my special friend,
my snowman named
just "Bob."

We laughed and sang
and ran about
as Bob began to be.
We gathered up
what we would need—
everything was free!

Some coal for eyes,
a carrot nose,
some sticks,
a scarf,
a hat—
a smile so wide
it warmed your heart,
a coat,
and that was that.

Perhaps you may think so far that magic ruled that day,
but so far will seem like nothing compared to what was on its way!

For this is when our new friend, Bob, decided to awake.

He opened up his twinkling eyes;

his belly, it did shake.

His voice, I do remember,
was something of a dream.
His countenance, so pleasing—
unearthly, it did seem.

And though you might be doubtful—
a talking friend made out of snow?
This is what we heard from Bob—
he wanted us to know:

"You've given me my eyes
so I might see and blink,
a mouth, a hat, a carrot nose
so I might speak and think.

"The scarf, indeed, is cozy,
it's sure to keep me warm,
and thank you all for giving me
such a shapely form!

"I hope it snows aplenty
so I might stay and share
in all your loving friendship,
your thoughtful, tender care.

"But when it warms or if in spring,
you miss that I'm not near,
put a sign in your front yard
that reads just: 'Bob was here.'"

Well, that was it . . .
'twas all Bob said
that dreamy, starry night.

He'd said his piece, he closed his eyes,
yet everything seemed right.